Little People of the Lost Coast

Eric Sterling, Secret Agent Series

ERIC STERLING
SECRET AGENT

Little People of the Lost Coast

ERNEST HERNDON

ZondervanPublishingHouse
Grand Rapids, Michigan

A Division of HarperCollinsPublishers

Little People of the Lost Coast

Copyright © 1997 by Ernest Herndon

Requests for information should be addressed to:

ZondervanPublishingHouse
Grand Rapids, Michigan 49530

Library of Congress Cataloging-in-Publication Data
  Herndon, Ernest.
  Little people of the lost coast / Ernest Herndon.
      p.   cm.—(Eric Sterling, secret agent ; #8)
  Summary: While river rafting and backpacking in Northern
California, Ax, Erik, and Sharon hear reports of gnomes in the remote
forest, leading to intrigue and danger for the group.
      ISBN: 0-310-20733-9 (pbk.)
      [1. Adventure and adventurers—Fiction.   2. Christian life—Fiction.
3. California—Fiction.]   I. Title.   II. Series: Herndon, Ernest.   Eric
Sterling, secret agent ; #8.
PZ7.H4318Li   1997
[Fic]—dc21   97–1622
                                                                              CIP
                                                                              AC

Interior illustrations by Gloria Oostema

Printed in the United States of America

97 98 99 00 01 02 03 04 /❖ DH/ 10 9 8 7 6 5 4 3

For Lucy

1

Miss Spice pulled the van into the gravel parking lot beside the American River. When we climbed out, the mountain air felt chilly.

"You kids wait here," she said. "I'll go see about a guide."

She walked toward a small building surrounded by rubber rafts and colorful kayaks.

"She seems to be having fun," Sharon said with a grin.

"You sure wouldn't think she's the director of a top spy agency," added Sharon's brother Ax.

Miss Spice was wearing blue jeans, hiking boots, and a flannel shirt. Her ginger-red hair was tied back in a ponytail which bounced as she walked.

"She looks too young for that," I agreed.

"And too cute," Sharon said.

"No cuter than you, Sis," Ax said, playfully tugging his sister's blond hair.

"Yeah, right."

Actually, Sharon *was* cute. She was freckled and tan from a long summer of adventure. Her brother—at thirteen, a year older than both of us—was even darker, since he practiced karate in the sun a lot.

Maybe Miss Spice didn't resemble a spy director, but if any kids looked like wildlife secret agents, Ax and Sharon did. They were outdoorsy and athletic. I was another story—just average. And not too happy about our plans right now.

"Man, listen to that river!" I said, frowning at the roar of fast water.

"Cool, huh?" Ax said.

"Cool? Ice cold is more like it—and deadly," I said.

"Oh, Eric, it'll be fun," Sharon said. "We've never been white-water rafting before."

"I don't remember ever wanting to," I said. "Do you think Miss Spice would mind if I stayed in the van?"

Sharon punched me in the arm. "Don't you dare say that around her. It'll break her heart!"

"Yeah," Ax said. "This is supposed to be a reward for all our hard work this summer."

Some reward. But we *had* worked hard, risking

our lives for Wildlife Special Investigations on missions around the world. Giant killer birds, deadly snakes, wolves, gators—I shuddered at the memories. Now, with school just a couple weeks away, Miss Spice thought she was doing us a favor by taking us white-water rafting in California.

"I'd rather be at home taking it easy," I muttered. "I've got a bunch of computer games I haven't even gotten to try out."

"You and that computer!" Ax snorted. "You need to get outside more."

"Outside? What do you think I've been doing all—"

"Shhh, you guys," Sharon said. "Here she comes."

Miss Spice walked out with a man whose brown hair was longer than hers. Despite the cold air, he wore only a headband, T-shirt, cutoff jean shorts, and river sandals.

"Kids, this is Far Out Johnson," Miss Spice said. "He's going to be our raft guide."

"What's happenin', kids?" the man said.

Sharon giggled. "Is your name really Far Out?"

"That's what they call me. Real name's Farley."

"This is Eric, Ax, and Sharon," Miss Spice said.

"Glad to meet you. I guess everybody can swim?" We nodded.

"Ever done any white water before?"

"I have," Miss Spice said, "but it's been a while."

"We've done some canoeing," I said.

"And sea kayaking," Ax added.

Far Out shook his head. "See that river? It would eat a sea kayak for lunch. And a canoe could only make it with lots of flotation. All right, let's get suited up. Go inside and they'll fit you out with some farmer johns. I'll get the boat and paddles. Meet me out here when you're ready."

"What's a farmer john?" I asked.

"Insulated wet suit. River's cold." He nodded toward a group of people putting a raft into the water. They all wore black wet suits with shoulder straps like overalls. "A full wet suit's really more than you need. Farmer john'll do the trick. You all got tennis shoes?"

"In the van," Miss Spice said.

"You'll need them."

We got our tennis shoes and went in the store. It was crammed with wet suits, paddles, life vests, and other outdoor gear. Classic rock played on a stereo. A blond lady popped her chewing gum and picked suits out to fit us.

"Is that 'In-a-Gadda-da-Vida'?" Miss Spice asked her.

"Yeah. Cool song, huh?"

"I haven't heard that in *ages*."

"The way they blend classical organ, kettle drums, and fuzz box is pretty timeless, don't ya think?" the saleslady said.

I snickered.

"What's funny?" said Ax.

"Old people's music," I whispered.

"Who's old?" demanded Miss Spice.

"You're crazy, Eric," Ax chimed in. "Iron Butterfly is cool."

"It's classic," Sharon agreed.

"Wrong," I retorted. "But I didn't mean to say you were old, Miss Spice. I mean, not real old."

"Gee, thanks," she said.

We went into dressing rooms to change. When we came out, that song was *still* on.

"I still say that's a goofy song," I told Ax as we walked outside.

"Not as goofy as you look," he said.

"Oh yeah? You make me think of a stork."

"Now boys," Miss Spice said. "We all look a bit silly, but when we get on the river we'll be glad we have them on."

The wet suit was skin-tight and felt funny. We wore our regular shirts under them, plus socks and tennis shoes.

"Sharon looks like a Martian figure skater," Ax whispered loud enough for her to hear.

"A few minutes ago you said I was cute," she said with a toss of her head.

"That was before you turned into a Martian." He gave his sister a shove, and she pushed him right back.

"Well, you're a Venusian," she said.

Miss Spice and I ignored them. At the riverside, Far Out stood by a big rubber raft, a batch of plastic paddles, and some life vests. He too had put on a wet suit.

"All right!" he said with a grin when we came up. "Ready for some action?"

"Yes!" said everyone but me.

He handed out the life vests. While we put them on, he slid the boat out. "Everybody in," he called.

We waded into the fast water.

"Ouch!" I said. "That's like ice!"

"Pure mountain water," Far Out said. "Just wait till you fall in."

"Fall in?" I said. "Who's falling in?"

He just grinned and shrugged.

Uh-oh.

2

"Some quick instructions," Far Out said, standing by the raft to hold it steady. "Sit on the sides with one knee in the center. The raft is self-bailing, which means it can't fill up. Now, I'm the raft captain, and when I give a command, you've got to do it right then, and fast. Okay?"

We nodded.

"When I say draw left, the people on the left side reach out with your paddles and draw them toward you. When I say draw right, the people on the right do the same. When I say straight ahead, that means just paddle straight. Everybody got it?"

"Uh, I'm not so sure about some of those strokes," I said.

"We'll get to practice a little before the first rapid." He pulled the raft out into the current and hopped in the back. "Everybody make sure your life vest is tight. Now let's try those strokes."

We had about thirty seconds to practice. Then Far Out stared downstream. "Rapid's coming up. Everybody in place." He had to talk loudly to be heard over the growing roar. My stomach tingled.

"Draw right!" Far Out yelled.

Ax and Sharon, who were on the right side, obeyed.

"Straight ahead!"

We all paddled.

"Stop!"

We lifted our paddles. The current had picked up a lot. We were speeding along like a car on an interstate. The landscape changed quickly as we shot downriver; rocky cliffs now rose on both sides, topped by evergreen trees. The roar kept getting louder.

I glanced back and saw that Far Out was frowning. He bit his lip and shook his head. "This one's tricky," he said, practically hollering now. "We're going to have to give it all we've got."

Oh no! My stomach didn't tingle anymore. It buzzed!

"Draw left!" Far Out shouted.

That was my side! Miss Spice and I dug our paddles in the water and scooped them toward us. It didn't seem to have any effect. The river was too strong.

"Harder! Harder!" Far Out yelled, digging his own paddle in.

The raft bounced up and down. Icy water splashed over me.

"Straight ahead! Draw left! Draw right! Draw left again! Quick!"

Water churned and pounded all around us. Any minute I expected to flip and drown. To our left was a huge rapid.

"Draw left left left!" Far Out yelled frantically.

Then we were past it. The river grew quiet. We had won!

"Rats!" Far Out said, shaking his head.

"What's the matter?" I asked.

"We missed the rapid."

"I thought that was the plan," I said.

Far Out grinned. "The plan is to *shoot* the rapids, boy! Not miss them."

"Yeah, dummy, why do you think we're out here?" Ax said to me.

"Uh—to survive?"

Everybody laughed. They were all soaking wet, like me, their hair plastered to their heads. But their eyes were bright with excitement.

"Oh, I forgot to tell you one thing," Far Out said as we drifted. "If you fall out, float on your back, feet first. That way your feet will bounce off the rocks."

I started to ask for details but he yelled, "Draw left!"

We moved the raft sideways toward a wave about the size of a sofa.

"It's surfing time!" Far Out said.

We guided the raft against the wave. Far Out pressed down on the rear, and somehow the water pressure held us in place. The rushing river surrounded us, but we weren't moving. It was weird and fun and dizzy, like the current was running backward. Far Out gave us a thumbs-up. Then he pushed off with his paddle, and the suction released us.

"Neat, huh?" Miss Spice said happily. We nodded.

"Haystacks coming up!" Far Out announced.

Downriver was a line of waves that resembled piles of hay. We hit one and dropped with a *thunk*!

"Cool!" Ax said.

We hit another one. *Thunk!*

"Not bad!" I said with a grin.

We approached the third one, bigger than the others. As we rode over the crest I waited for the *thunk*! Instead I heard *splash*—and I was in the river! We'd hit so hard I bounced right off the raft.

Except for my leg. It was caught on something, or someone had grabbed it. The river held me under, and I was being dragged along, pinned under the raft. I tried to pull free but whatever held my leg wouldn't let go!

3

Cold water filled my eyes, nose, and ears. The heavy rubber raft scraped against my forehead, pushing me deeper. My heart pounded and I couldn't breathe!

Suddenly my leg came free.

I thrashed away from the raft. As my head came up I sucked in air. *Ahhh!*

As the current carried me along, I remembered what Far Out had said. I stretched out on my back with my feet downriver. The life vest held me up. This wasn't so bad. Kind of restful. Then somebody shouted, "Swim to the bank!"

I looked back and saw Far Out, Ax, and Sharon waving me ashore. I heard a roar downstream and realized I was heading for another rapid! My adrenaline kicked into gear again and I swam hard. I made it to the rocky shore just in time.

Then I noticed Miss Spice on the bank a short distance upriver. She grinned and waved. I guessed she had gotten thrown out too.

The raft floated down, picked her up, then got me. Far Out beached for a rest.

"How do you like haystacks now, Eric?" he asked with a grin.

"I'm not sure what happened."

"I grabbed your leg," Ax said. "I thought I could pull you back in. Far Out told me to let go. Sorry."

"Miss Spice fell out the same time you did," Sharon said. "Your side of the raft went straight up in the air. The rest of us held on."

"It felt like the time I got thrown by a horse," Miss Spice said.

"How'd you like swimming?" Far Out asked us.

"Fun!" Miss Spice said.

I shrugged. "I didn't mind."

And really, I didn't. In fact, I was almost glad it happened. Now I knew the river wasn't totally deadly. Even if you fell out in the middle of a rapid, like I did, it wasn't the end of the world.

"What was it like?" Ax asked me. I could tell he was jealous.

"It was scary at first when I couldn't get air. Then I just lay back and floated."

"Why didn't you swim ashore?"

"Guess I forgot. I was trying to float on my back with my feet downstream, like Far Out said."

Far Out pushed us away from the bank. I wasn't so scared anymore. I knew I could handle it. Even when we got to the biggest rapid on the river, it was more fun than frightening. We roared around a sharp bend and dropped so fast that water poured all over us. Then we bounced several times until we were in still water again.

It was late afternoon when we reached the boat landing. A flatbed truck was waiting. We loaded everything up. Far Out, Miss Spice, and the driver rode in front and the rest of us in back. The air didn't feel so cold anymore. It smelled like a Christmas tree.

"What do you guys think about white-water rafting?" Sharon asked.

"I love it!" Ax said. "I can't wait till tomorrow when we do it again."

"It's kind of like a wet roller coaster," I said. "But I've never been crazy about roller coasters."

"What about you, Sharon?" Ax asked.

She grinned. "Next time *I* want to fall out."

"Yeah! Me too!" Ax said.

I laughed. "You guys are crazy."

Back at the outfitter we changed into dry clothes and got back in the van. "There's a public campground not far from here," Miss Spice said. "We'll stop somewhere and eat supper, then go make camp."

Along the highway we found a restaurant that looked like a big log cabin. After we ordered, Miss Spice went to the lobby and got a newspaper.

"So what's in the news?" I asked.

She held up the thin newspaper. "Not much. This is just a small local weekly." She spread it on the table and read us the headlines: "Lula Jones Celebrates 80th Birthday. Cow Has Twins for Second Year. 4-H Contest Winners Announced. Three Arrested for Marijuana Possession. Gnomes Spotted in Desolation Wilderness."

"Huh?" Ax said. "Gnomes?"

"That's what it says. Listen: 'A pair of backpackers reported sighting a couple of so-called gnomes in the Desolation Wilderness Area last week. Billy Martin and his wife Sally, both of San Francisco, swear they saw two tiny people running into the forest. "They were too small to be humans," Martin said. "They couldn't even have been dwarfs, in my opinion." As proof he showed photos taken of footprints in the snow.'"

Miss Spice showed us the paper. "Here's the photo."

It wasn't a very good picture. It was black and white and showed a person's hand positioned for scale beside smudges that might have been tiny footprints.

"I can't believe they print something like that," Ax said. "That's nothing but a hoax."

"Maybe it was just little kids," I said with a shrug.

"Those could even be bobcat tracks or something," Sharon said.

"It would be fun to go check it out, though, wouldn't it?" Miss Spice said.

"What do you mean?" Ax asked.

"The Desolation Wilderness isn't far from here. And I noticed the place where we rented the raft has backpacks. We could hike up there tomorrow instead of rafting."

"That's a great idea!" I said.

"You just don't want to raft," Ax said to me.

He was right, of course.

Miss Spice smiled. "When I was little, we lived in the country, and sometimes at night we heard funny noises coming from the woods. My father used to tell me they were gnomes singing."

"Really?" I said.

She nodded. "He was just kidding. I think they were wood ducks, which made a funny noise kind of like human voices at night. But the idea of gnomes always enchanted me."

She shrugged as the waitress brought our food. "We can raft the American again, like we had planned, or hike into the Desolation Wilderness. Since we've done a day of rafting, I thought it might be fun to try something different. What do you say?"

"I say we hike," I said.

"Sounds fun to me," Sharon said.

Ax frowned. "Looks like I'm out-voted."

"You'll like it," Miss Spice told him. "From what I've read, the Desolation Wilderness is pretty wild."

Our waitress finished setting our plates down. "They don't call it Desolation for nothing, honey," she said.

4

An hour into our hike the next morning, I regretted my choice. Floating along on a raft seemed like a piece of cake compared to this.

"Hey, you guys, this is hard work!" I said when we stopped for a rest.

"The mountains are pretty, though, aren't they?" Miss Spice said, waving her arms at peaks all around.

"Yeah, but this trail is all uphill," I complained.

"Told you we should have gone rafting," Ax said. "Not that hiking bothers me."

"Yeah, nothing bothers you," I said.

"I'll tell you what bothers me," he said. "You got to fall out and I didn't."

"*Got* to fall out? You act like I wanted to. I could have drowned."

"He's jealous because you had a near-death experience and he didn't," Sharon said.

"I would gladly have traded places with you, Ax," Miss Spice said, trying to make peace. "Now we need to enjoy our surroundings. Doesn't that breeze feel delightful?"

"Cold, if you ask me," I said. "It wasn't so bad down in the parking lot."

"Just wait till we get up there," Ax said. He nodded toward the top of the mountain, which looked miles away.

"We're not going that far, are we, Miss Spice?" I asked.

"I thought we'd go to the other side and make camp," she said.

I groaned.

"Let's do it," Ax said.

"Eric, put on your jacket if you're cold," Miss Spice told me.

I put on my jean jacket. It was a good thing I did, because the higher we went, the chillier it got.

The trail zigzagged up the mountainside. There weren't many trees, so there was little to block the wind—but the views *were* pretty. I tried pretending I was a frontiersman back in the old days, headed into Indian country. Then I remembered that frontiersmen had horses to carry their gear and buffalo-skin coats to keep them warm—not backpacks and jean jackets.

We stopped for lunch on a big, flat boulder, then napped in the sunshine. But gray clouds rolled in and the air got colder, so we hit the trail again. Then we noticed a white dust in the air.

"Snow!" I said.

"Doesn't feel cold enough for snow," Ax said as he stopped to put on a windbreaker.

"And this is August!" Sharon said. "I mean, it's summertime."

"Elevation," said Miss Spice. "At these altitudes it can snow anytime."

The powder flew thicker and faster. Soon it blocked our view of the mountains.

"This is a blizzard!" Miss Spice called happily as she led the way up the trail.

"Neat!" Ax said, enjoying himself at last. "Who'd have thought we'd get a snowstorm during summer vacation?"

I would have thought a blizzard would be freezing cold, but it really wasn't. My jacket, along with the exercise, kept me pretty warm. All in all this wasn't so bad.

By the time we reached the top, the snow had almost stopped. The ground was covered in white. We hiked along a flat stretch, then downhill. A snowy field with some twisted trees lay before us, with new views of mountains. Down below was a lake surrounded by forest. In the distance lay another lake, much bigger. Miss Spice got out her map.

"That big one is Lake Tahoe," she said, "a big tourist resort."

"This is beautiful!" Sharon said, sniffing the crisp air.

"We'll camp up there where it's flat," Miss Spice said. "There's lots of snow so we can look for tracks."

Ax frowned. "Tracks? Oh yeah, gnomes." He snickered.

"You don't have to look, Ax," Sharon said. "But *I'm* going to. We might find something interesting."

We pitched our two tents in the snow and gathered firewood. Then we spread out to look.

"Don't go far," Miss Spice told us as we separated. "I don't want anybody getting lost."

There wasn't much chance of that since we could see for a long way. As I walked along, the sun peeked through. Its light reflected off the clouds and snow and turned everything pink.

"Hey, Eric!" Ax called. "Look at this!"

I hurried over. He was staring at the pink snow.

"It's a little human footprint," he said. "No joke!"

I scoffed. "Oh, come on, Ax. Even I know a raccoon track when I see one."

"Raccoon! Are you sure?"

"Of course. See how the thumb goes? And the claws? But look over here! A boot print. I wonder who made it?"

"Uh—I'd say a man in a red-and-black checkered hunting shirt carrying a rifle," Ax said.

"Yeah, right. And how would you know all that?"

"Because he's standing over there watching us!"

5

I looked up as the man stepped toward us. In addition to the lumberjack shirt, he wore a goofy purple hat with a short brim. His pants were stuffed into mukluks with fake fur sticking out the top. He looked like a city slicker trying to be a woodsman.

"What are you boys doing out here?" he demanded in a voice that reminded me of a school-teacher. The look he gave Ax and me made me feel like he'd caught us in the hall without a pass. At least his gun barrel was pointed at the ground and not at us.

"Just camping, sir," I said. "We're not trying to bother anybody."

"Are you hunting?" Ax asked, trying to be friendly.

"Hunting! What do you mean, hunting?"

Ax shrugged. "Well, you *are* carrying a gun."

"Oh, this." He laughed, but it sounded phony. "I just carry this for protection."

"From what—gnomes?" Ax grinned.

The man's smile faded. "What do you know about gnomes?"

"Nothing!" Ax stammered. "We just read about them in the paper, that's all."

"You haven't seen any, have you?"

"Nothing but these tracks here, and they're from a raccoon," Ax said.

The man glanced at the prints, then nodded. "All right then, no harm done." He smiled again. "Name's Dwayne. What's yours?"

"I'm Ax. He's Eric."

"Camped near here, are you?"

"Yes sir," I said.

"I'm down by the lake. Just fishing, that's all." He peered at the sky. "In fact, I'd better be heading back. It's getting late."

He clumped away in the snow, then stopped and came back. "Forgot my walking stick," he muttered, retrieving a staff he had left leaning against a tree.

"Man, what a weird dude," Ax said after the man disappeared.

"Somehow I don't think he's really a fisherman," I said.

"Or a hunter either."

"What's he doing out here, then?" I asked.

"Beats me," Ax said. "I'm just glad he's not camped near us."

"Me too. Well, let's go get a fire going. It's turning cold."

"Wait a minute," Ax said. "Do you think we shouldn't tell Sharon and Miss Spice about that guy?"

"Why not?"

"It might spook them. You know how women are."

"Oh, come on, Ax. They're as brave as we are."

He shrugged, and we headed back to camp. We had a crackling campfire going when Miss Spice and Sharon showed up. Sharon reported finding bobcat tracks, while Miss Spice said she saw lots of rabbit sign. We told them about the raccoon prints and then about Dwayne, but we didn't go into detail, just said we'd bumped into a local fisherman.

It was a good thing we had warm sleeping bags, because it really got cold that night. Next day we broke camp and then hiked back down the way we'd come. We rested a bit and then turned in our rented packs at the outfitter.

"It's too late to do any rafting today," Miss Spice said as we drove toward town. "We'll get something to eat—but first I want to stop by the newspaper office."

"What for?" Ax asked.

"I thought they'd like to know about our gnome research."

Ax and I looked at each other and shook our heads. And people said kids were silly!

The newspaper office was a concrete-block building in a small mountain town. Inside, an old lady sat at a cluttered desk doing paperwork.

"Can I help you?" she growled when we came in.

"Hi," Miss Spice said. "We just came from the Desolation Wilderness. We saw your article on gnomes, and went to—"

"Don't tell me. You didn't see a thing."

"Uh, right," said Miss Spice.

"So now you want me to admit it was all a tall tale, is that it?" Before we could answer, she reached into a drawer and pulled out some photos, handing them to Miss Spice. We crowded around to stare. They plainly showed tiny human shoe prints in the snow, just a few inches long!

"Wow! It didn't look this clear in the paper," Ax said.

"This ain't the *New York Times*, sugar," the lady said.

"Couldn't these be children's footprints?" Sharon asked.

"They'd have to be toddlers, almost," the woman replied. "And what would children that young be doing out in those mountains? Besides, the couple swore they saw gnomes—little people, leprechauns,

31

call them what you will—and they seemed like honest folks to me."

"This is truly amazing," Miss Spice said, handing the photos back. "We just went up on a lark. We didn't really expect to find anything."

"You should have stopped by here first, honey. I could have saved you a trip," the woman said.

"How so?"

"After that couple came down, people got curious. Some even went up there looking. Nobody could find a thing. I'm certain they spooked the little people."

I nodded. "Like that Dwayne guy."

"Who?" Miss Spice asked.

"That fisherman," I said.

"Or so he said," Ax added.

The newswoman stared at us quizzically.

"Ax and I met this man up there when we were looking for tracks," I said. "Looked like a hunter. Had a rifle and everything."

"Why didn't you tell us that?" Sharon said. "About the rifle, I mean."

"We didn't want you to worry," Ax said.

"Ha!" said Sharon, indignantly.

"He claimed to be a fisherman," I said. "Said he was carrying the rifle for protection."

"Could be," the newswoman said. "People fish up there this time of year, and there are bears. Then again, maybe he was hunting out of season."

Ax nodded. "He acted kind of suspicious."

"But where would the gnomes have gone?" Sharon asked.

"Oh, there's plenty of places for them to hide in those mountains, sweetie," the newslady said. "But here's a new development." She handed us a newspaper from her desk. "The Mendocino paper, yesterday's edition."

Miss Spice took the paper and read aloud: "Gnome-Sighting Reported at Lost Coast." She looked up. "But that's halfway across the state!"

"Surely it's not the same ones," Sharon said.

The woman stubbed out her stinky cigarette. "Of course not. How would they get there, a gnome-mobile?" She laughed, then began to cough. She doubled over, hacking. Finally she caught her breath and sat up. "If you really want to see a gnome, I'd suggest you go to the Lost Coast. But you'd better go fast, before *they* get spooked, too."

We thanked her for her time and left. Miss Spice looked thoughtful as we drove to the restaurant. "You know, I've got relatives in Mendocino," she said.

"Wait a minute," Ax said. "What about rafting?"

"This is such an opportunity," Miss Spice said. "I'm not sure we should pass it up."

"Where's the Lost Coast?" I asked. "It's not another 10,000-foot mountain, I hope."

"It's north of Mendocino, where the highway veers away from the coast," Miss Spice said. "It's very remote, which is why they call it lost."

"Oh, boy!" Sharon said. "I've seen pictures of the north coast of California. It's awesome! Big cliffs with waves crashing in. Giant redwood trees. And lots of seals!"

Miss Spice nodded. "We could drive to Mendocino tomorrow, eat lunch at my cousin's restaurant, then go on up to the Lost Coast and take a look."

"I don't believe this," Ax said. "Now I'll never get to find out what it's like to swim in white water."

I laughed. "Man, you're crazy."

He snorted. "You guys are searching for leprechauns, and you call me crazy?"

6

"Miss Spice, do you *really* believe in gnomes?" Sharon asked at breakfast in the restaurant. We had spent the night in the campground and would soon make the drive to Mendocino.

"No," Miss Spice said, a twinkle in her eye. "But I haven't ruled out the possibility."

"Oh, come on, Miss Spice!" Ax said, munching a piece of toast. "I mean, you're the director of WSI. How can you believe in leprechauns?"

She sipped her coffee. "How do you know they *don't* exist, Ax?"

"Everybody knows, that's why!"

"Everybody once knew the world was flat, too—or so they thought," Miss Spice said.

Sharon and I snickered.

"What about Bigfoot?" Ax asked. "Do you believe in that?"

"Actually, there are all sorts of creatures which people say exist but which haven't been proven," Miss Spice said. "Bigfoot is one. The *yeti*, also known as the abominable snowman. *M'kele m'bembe*, the Congo dinosaur. And so on. Plus, you know giants are mentioned in the Bible."

"Yeah, Goliath," Sharon said.

Miss Spice nodded. "Also the Nephilim. They're mentioned in Genesis."

"What is a gnome, anyway?" I asked. "Is it really the same as a leprechaun?"

Miss Spice smiled. "I read books about all that when I was a girl. As I recall, gnomes and leprechauns are basically similar. They're very small, very shy, and live deep in the forest away from people."

"That's not the same as a dwarf, is it?" I asked.

"No, dwarves are just abnormally short people."

"What about elves?" Ax asked.

Miss Spice shook her head. "Elves are like fairies, little magical beings that fly around and disappear. Strictly make-believe."

"Ah ha!" Ax said. "But how do you know they *don't* exist?"

Miss Spice laughed. "Good point. But we haven't seen any photos of elf footprints. Look, I don't want you guys to get the wrong idea. I don't *really* believe in gnomes, okay? It's just that nowadays it seems like nobody believes in anything wonderful or mysterious anymore. All I'm saying is that God's world is a lot bigger and more exciting than we tend to think."

"I think those photos are worth checking out," Sharon said, nodding.

"I'd rather see Bigfoot," Ax said, finishing his meal and wiping his mouth with a napkin. "Or maybe one of those Nephilim!"

Miss Spice phoned her cousin in Mendocino to let her know we were coming. Then we loaded up in the van and set off on our journey. We drove down through the mountains to flat farmland. Then we entered hill country with vineyards and wineries. At last we came to Highway 1 which ran along the coast. On our left, the Pacific Ocean banged against the rocks. Nice view.

It was early afternoon when we got to Mendocino. It was a little town with narrow streets and old-time buildings instead of malls and shopping centers. Miss Spice parked in front of a brick building with big glass windows painted with the words "North Coast Ice Cream and Pastry Shop."

"This is my cousin Sarah's place," Miss Spice said. "Anybody hungry?"

"Yes!" Ax said.

As we got out and walked toward the door, a girl came gliding down the sidewalk on in-line skates.

She wore a helmet and earphones over her long brown hair. She was dressed in pink shorts, white T-shirt, kneepads, and kneesocks. She stopped when she saw us and stared at Miss Spice.

"Meg?" Miss Spice said.

"Aunt Jane?" The girl's face brightened.

Miss Spice chuckled. "I'm your cousin, but that's what you always called me when you were little."

They hugged. "Come on in and see Mom," Meg said.

"I can't believe how much you've grown!" Miss Spice said as we all went in.

The place smelled sweet, like doughnuts. There were dirty dishes on some of the tables, but no one was around except a woman at the cash register counting change. She was tall and thin with brown hair like Meg's.

"Sarah!" Miss Spice said.

"Jane!" They hugged and squealed and laughed while Meg stood grinning. Sarah wore a blue shirt, black sweatpants, black socks, and sandals. Her perfume smelled like incense.

"Sarah, Meg, these are my friends Ax, his sister Sharon, and Eric," Miss Spice said.

"So glad to meet you," Sarah said. "Please excuse the wreck in here. There was an Organic Growers Association meeting, and I haven't had time to clean up. My help is already gone." She brushed back a strand of hair.

"This is my beloved, hard-working cousin Sarah and her dear daughter Meg," Miss Spice said.

"My dear daughter Meg is running late," Sarah said. "We've got dishes to wash, young lady."

"We'll all help," Miss Spice said.

"Heavens no. They can wait," Sarah said. "How about some pastries? I've got plenty left from this morning."

"Are you sure?"

"Absolutely!"

We sat down at a big table. Meg, in stocking feet now, brought us glasses of ice water while Sarah carried in a huge platter of goodies, like doughnuts and cinnamon rolls and muffins.

"Everything's organic," said Sarah, smiling.

"You two sit down and join us, please," Miss Spice said.

Sarah wiped her forehead with the back of her arm. "I'm easily persuaded," she said, taking a chair. "How was your trip? You made good time."

"We're on the trail of some gnomes," Miss Spice said with a grin.

"You mentioned something about that on the phone," Sarah said. "I didn't quite follow."

"Don't you read your own newspaper? It says gnomes were seen on the Lost Coast."

"I'm not much into newspapers," Sarah said. "You know I tuned in, turned on, and dropped out a long time ago."

Miss Spice smiled. "Some of us have come back to reality, though, dear."

"Reality? You're looking for gnomes and you talk about reality?"

The women laughed.

"Why don't you come with us?" Miss Spice said.

"Too much work. Wish I could. Meg might like to go."

Meg scrunched up her face and examined us. "You guys are going to look for gnomes?"

Miss Spice nodded.

"Like, how?"

"I thought we would hike in, make camp, and just scout around some."

"My sister here is pretty good at tracks," Ax said. "She knows all kinds of things about wildlife and stuff."

Meg turned to Ax. She smiled, and her big brown eyes brightened. "Sure," she said. "I'll go."

7

We arrived at the Lost Coast campground late in the afternoon. A few tents stood among tall trees and picnic tables.

As we got out of the van and stretched, Miss Spice glanced at her watch. "We've got a few hours before dark," she said. "Think we should camp here or hike in a little ways?"

"Let's hike!" Ax said. Then he added in a low voice, "The sooner we get through with this, the sooner we can go rafting."

"You like to raft?" Meg asked him.

"You bet!"

"All right," Miss Spice said. "Let's load up and go."

"Ever try kayaking?" Meg asked Ax as we pulled our packs out of the van and began putting them on.

"Only sea kayaking," Ax said. "I've never been white-water kayaking."

"You've been sea kayaking?" Meg said. "Cool! Mom won't let me go. She says it's too dangerous."

"We didn't exactly go in heavy surf," I said.

Ax gave me a dirty look. "It was still pretty dangerous," he said. "We were in the Gulf of Mexico chasing wolfnappers."

"Wolfnappers? Gosh!" Meg acted like Ax had captured them single-handedly. Sharon and I looked at each other and shook our heads.

"This way, gang," Miss Spice said, leading the way to the mossy trail that led into the forest. Sharon and I followed, while Meg and Ax brought up the rear.

"Maybe when we get back you can teach me something about sea kayaking," Meg said.

"Sure! And I'd like to try in-line skating, like you were doing," Ax said. "I'll bet it's good for your balance."

"Are you into gymnastics or something?" Meg asked.

"Karate."

"He's a black belt," Sharon called over her shoulder.

"Really?" Meg said. "What style?"

"Tang Soo Do," Ax answered modestly.

"Cool. I do Aikido. A little, anyway."

"Aikido! No joke? I've never met anybody who did that. I've seen it in the movies, though."

"It's not really like it looks in the movies," Meg said. "Not what I know, anyway."

"I know what you mean," Ax said. "Martial art movies are fun, but they're pretty stupid. Maybe you could show me some Aikido moves later."

"Okay. And you can show me some—what did you call it?"

"Tang Soo Do."

I tried to tune them out. They obviously weren't going to shut up. They were like two songbirds—or lovebirds, more like it.

I focused on the woods. Most of the trees were average size, but a few were really big.

"Are those redwoods?" I asked Miss Spice.

"Yes," she said. "These woods have been logged before, but the loggers left a few old ones standing."

"I can see why people think gnomes live here," Sharon said in a hushed voice. "There's something magical about it."

"Look up here, kids," Miss Spice said.

We had been going mostly uphill. Now the woods opened onto a big grassy cliff. I could hear surf pounding and I felt mist on my face.

The trail led us near the edge of the cliff, and there before us was the ocean. The sky was cloudy but one or two rays of sun peeked out, and it made the sea look like metal. In the distance, that is. Up close it was a bunch of big waves bashing the rocks. No wonder Meg's mom wouldn't let her kayak in this stuff!

"Look down there! Pelicans!" Sharon said.

The birds skimmed low, just over the whitecaps.

"They're sure cutting it close," I said.

"They're looking for fish to scoop up in their pouches," Sharon said.

"Maybe we'll see some seals," Meg said, joining us.

"I hope so!" Sharon said.

"We saw some manatees once," Ax told her.

"Really?" Meg said. "Where?"

Here they go again, I thought.

For a while the trail followed the edge of the cliffs. Then it turned back into the forest. It zigzagged down a steep hill to a tiny creek. Part of the way up the other side was a flat camping area.

"What do you think?" Miss Spice said.

"Looks great!" I said. I was tired and ready to stop.

"Yeah," Sharon said. "It'll be neat to follow that creek down to the sea."

Ax and Meg came up. "Looks good," Ax said, as if he were scoutmaster or something.

"All right, then," Miss Spice said, shedding her pack. "Ax, you and Meg round up some firewood. Eric, you and Sharon pitch the tents. I'll start supper. Then we'll plot our strategy."

8

"This wood is too wet to burn!" Ax complained. He wiped his forehead, kneeling beside a pile of wood he and Meg had brought up.

"It rains here a lot," Meg said. "We're just lucky it's not raining now."

Miss Spice, sitting by the camp stove next to a steaming pot, went to her pack. "Try one of these fire-starters," she said, tossing a stick to Ax.

"What is it?" He held it up with a curious frown.

"Compressed wood soaked with paraffin, I think. It burns a long time, so it's good for starting wet wood."

"Thanks."

Sharon and I finished staking out the two tents

and went over to watch. Ax lit the rectangular stick and arranged twigs over it like a teepee. They quickly began to smoke. Meg added slightly larger sticks until they had a fire going.

"It's not going to be a bonfire, but it's better than nothing," Ax said, leaning over to blow on the small flame to make it bigger.

"This spaghetti is just about ready," Miss Spice said. "Anybody hungry?"

"Me!"

"Yes!"

"I am!"

She laughed as we got our plates. She dished up the spicy-smelling food, and we sat around on logs and rocks eating.

"This is great, Miss Spice," Ax said, and the rest of us nodded.

An early star twinkled through the mist, but otherwise the sky was mostly cloudy. The air smelled of camp smoke, and in the distance we could hear the surf, like kids whispering in their bunks.

"Boy, this is great!" Meg said. "I don't ever get to go camping. Mom's too busy with the shop to get away."

"These kids are old pros," Miss Spice said. "They've camped all over the world."

"Really?"

Miss Spice looked at Sharon, Ax and me. "Think I should tell her?"

We nodded.

"We work for WSI," Miss Spice told Meg. "That's Wildlife Special Investigations, a branch of the CIA."

"She's our boss," Sharon said.

Meg stared at us. "You mean you're, like, secret agents?"

We nodded.

"Cool!" Then she peered at her cousin as if seeing her in a new light. "I remember Mom telling me you worked for the government. I had no idea it was the CIA, though."

"She's the director," Ax said proudly.

"Of WSI, not the whole CIA," Miss Spice added with a smile. "The kids' camping trips have actually been assignments."

"Is this an assignment now?" Meg asked.

"Just a vacation."

"But it's kind of turning into an assignment, with the gnomes," I said.

"Weird," Meg said.

"They've seen some pretty strange things," Miss Spice said. "Like a thirty-foot monitor lizard."

"Thirty foot!"

Sharon nodded. "It was on the island of Baru, in the South Pacific. Scientists were breeding giant mutant lizards. We got to ride one."

"It didn't try to eat you?" Meg said.

Sharon shook her head. "It was friendly."

"Because I saw a great white shark one time, and

it would eat you in one bite, almost," Meg said.

"What happened?" Ax asked her.

"For a field trip our teacher took us to see this biologist. He had a surfboard with a camera in it. He would reel the surfboard in with a giant rod and reel, like, and he'd make it twitch. The idea was to make a great white attack. And it did."

"You saw it?" Sharon said.

"Well, it was a long way out, but we saw the surfboard go up in the air and then come down, and then we saw the fin. It was huge! Later we got to see the video. You could see the shark swimming straight up with its mouth open and the teeth showing and everything."

"Where was this?" I asked.

"Between here and Mendocino."

"In other words, not far from here," I said.

"Right."

"Remind me not to go swimming."

"Come on, let's wash these dishes," Miss Spice said, "before it's too dark."

We all went down to the stream and scrubbed the dishes with sand. Then we returned to the fire and built it up. It was nearly night.

"What about Bigfoot?" Sharon asked Meg. "Isn't he supposed to live up here?"

She shrugged. "That's what they say. I don't really believe in that kind of stuff."

"There were giants once, though," Ax said. "It says so in the Bible. What did you call them, Miss Spice?"

"Nephilim."

Ax nodded. "They were like superheroes in the olden days."

Miss Spice smiled. "I know! I'll get my Bible and read you that part."

She went to her pack and came back with the book and a flashlight. "I always carry a Bible camping," she said. "You never know when you'll get rained in and have to spend a lot of time in your tent." She opened it and shined her flashlight on the pages. "Let's see, Genesis chapter 6. 'The Nephilim were on the earth in those days—and also afterward—when the sons of God went to the daughters of men and had children by them. They were the heroes of old, men of renown.'" She flipped some pages. "And over here, in Numbers, it says the Israelites felt like grasshoppers compared to the Nephilim."

"Cool, huh?" Ax said.

"I never heard all that before," Meg said as Miss Spice went to put her Bible away. "We don't read the Bible. Mom said it's got too much negative energy."

"Negative energy?" Ax said, surprised.

"Yeah. All that stuff about hell and everything. You guys must be into it, huh?"

"We're Christians," Sharon said, nodding.

"Mom said Jesus was a great teacher," Meg said, poking the fire with a stick. "Kind of like Ram Baba. That's who we believe in."

9

Ax stared at Meg. "You believe in what?"

"Ram Baba. He lives in India. Mom says every so often God puts his spirit in a human, and now it's in Ram Baba. He teaches peace and love."

"So did Jesus," Ax said, "only he was saying it two thousand years ago."

"Ram Baba performs miracles," Meg said.

"So did Jesus," Ax retorted, "only he did *real* miracles."

"Ram Baba's are real!" Meg said. They were sounding angry.

Miss Spice returned. "You guys talking about Ram Baba?"

"How did you know about him?" I asked.

She smiled. "Sarah and I have had this conversation before." She sat down. "See, Meg's mother was raised in a very strict church environment back in Indiana. Like a lot of teenagers, she rebelled. Dropped out of church, moved to California. I hope and believe that someday she'll return to church, but she's entitled to her beliefs, and so is Meg."

"But that Ram Baba stuff sounds like some kind of cult!" Ax said.

"Well, your religion started out that way," Meg said.

"It did not!" Ax said.

Meg stood up. "And all that stuff about giants is stupid. This whole trip is stupid!" She ran to a tent.

"You can't call the Bible stupid!" Ax yelled.

"Ax, hush!" Miss Spice hissed. "Meg is our guest on this trip. And you may be one of the few Christian kids she knows, did you think of that? What kind of example are you setting?"

She went to the tent to comfort Meg.

"I think she's crying," Sharon said.

"It's not my fault," Ax said. "She insulted the Bible."

"You insulted *her* religion," Sharon said.

"Yeah, but it's wrong, and ours is right!"

"Maybe so," Sharon said, suddenly angry. "But *you're* wrong to be so rude to Meg." She stood up and went to the tent too.

"Way to go, Ax," I said.

"You too?"

"How can you convert somebody if you insult them?"

"I didn't mean to insult her. But *she* insulted *me*," he said.

I added a stick to the fire. "I don't think she meant to. Not at first, anyway."

"I knew this trip was bad news," Ax muttered. "All I wanted to do was go white-water rafting—not hunt for gnomes or argue with some silly girl."

Miss Spice returned. "Meg and Sharon have gone to bed," she said quietly. "I'm going to do the same."

"Miss Spice, I didn't mean to hurt her feelings," Ax said.

"Maybe you should tell her that."

He frowned. "I think she needs to apologize first."

Miss Spice shook her head sadly. "Good night, boys."

"Good night," we said.

"I guess I might as well turn in, too," I told Ax as Miss Spice left.

"You go ahead," he said, poking the fire and making sparks shower upward. "I'll be there in a while."

I went to the tent. I really felt bad about all this. Ax and Meg had really liked each other! Now they were bitter enemies.

Snug in my sleeping bag, I didn't hear Ax come to bed. Sometime in the night I did hear it start raining, though. Not much, just a drizzle.

Morning looked gloomy. We stood around in our ponchos eating oatmeal. Nobody said much. Ax and Meg never looked at each other, and Sharon seemed grumpy. Miss Spice tried to perk us up.

"All right, gang!" she said after we finished washing our breakfast dishes. "We're going to have fun today, rain or shine. This is our day to hunt gnomes, and we're not going to let a little drizzle stop us, are we?"

No one answered.

"I said are we?" she repeated.

"No ma'am," we mumbled.

"All right, here's the plan. We'll split up into teams. Ax, you and Eric follow the trail. Sharon, you and Meg take this creek. I'll go back the way we came. Let's make it a game. Whichever team identifies the most animal tracks wins. The losers have to wash dishes tonight."

"But it's raining," Ax grumbled. "All the tracks will be washed out."

"Look at it this way," Miss Spice said. "If you see a track, it's bound to be fresh."

"What if we see one but can't identify it?" I said.

"You've got to. That's the rule," Miss Spice answered.

"That's no fair," I said. "Sharon knows animal tracks better than we do."

Meg turned to Sharon. "Boys sure are whiners,

aren't they?"

I shut up.

"We'll meet back here at noon," Miss Spice said. "Don't anybody get lost. Ax and Eric, that means stay on the trail. Sharon and Meg, keep next to the stream. Okay, everybody?"

"Okay," we said.

Ax and I turned to walk down the trail. Then he stopped and pulled off his poncho. "I'm not taking this. It just gets in the way. Besides, it's barely raining."

I nodded and did the same. We hung the ponchos on branches by the tent. Then Ax led the way on the trail, uphill.

Soon my heart was pounding. "Not so fast, Ax!" I called. "This isn't a race! Besides, we're supposed to be looking for tracks."

He snorted. "What a joke. I'm not playing some dumb game, and I'm sure not looking for gnomes. I just want to hike, get some exercise."

We topped a ridge, our footsteps muffled on the ground cover. Trees rose in the mist around us, and raindrops dripped from the branches. It was kind of spooky.

Then the trail zigzagged down the hillside and entered a grassy valley.

"We ought to slow down," I said. "We might see some wildlife."

Ax stopped. "Listen! Hear that?"

"Running water?"

He pointed to a big, lonely tree. "There's a creek over there. Sounds like fast water. Let's check it out."

I grabbed his arm. "Ax!" I hissed. "Look!"

Someone stepped out from behind the tree. Someone tiny. Very tiny.

"A gnome!" Ax whispered.

10

It was the last thing I expected. Sure, I had seen the photos. Sure, I knew it was possible. But I didn't really expect to *see* one!

Not that I could tell much from this distance, especially through the mist. What I *could* tell was that he was tiny, like maybe two or three feet tall. He was walking along the creek bank, glancing over his shoulder. His face looked dark, as if he had a black beard instead of the long white one I would have expected, if I'd expected to see a gnome in the first place. Maybe he was a young gnome.

"What do we do?" Ax whispered.

"Don't move," I whispered back. "He doesn't see us."

Luckily the little guy wasn't looking in our direction. He seemed nervous, like something was trailing him.

We watched him continue down the creek and disappear into the forest.

"Man! I can't wait to tell Meg!" Ax said, eyes shining. He'd forgotten about being angry.

He turned to me. "Should we try to catch him?"

"Let's see where he goes."

We ran to the tree where we had spotted him. Little-bitty shoe prints showed plainly in the fresh mud.

"I wish I had a camera!" I said.

"That's why we've got to find him," Ax said. "Otherwise no one will ever believe us."

"Come on! But be quiet."

"All right. Hey, check out this creek!"

Right below us, down a steep bank, tumbled a white-water stream.

"That's wilder than the American River!" Ax said.

"Yeah, but too small to raft. Come on, let's track that gnome."

"Ouch!" He twisted. "Something stung me!"

I looked at his back, which he was trying to rub, and saw a flash of silver. I recognized it at once: a tranquilizer dart like scientists use to capture animals.

Ax's legs buckled. Before I could grab him he toppled off the bank and fell straight into the river!

I started to duck behind the tree, but I was too late. A sharp pain pricked my shoulder blade. I reached around to knock the dart out, but my muscles got weak. A wave of darkness swept over me, and I felt myself stumble backward. Then I was falling—straight into the icy water!

I went under all the way, but even the shock could barely wake me. I thrashed to the surface and gasped for air in slow motion. The current was sweeping me downstream just like it had in the American River—only this time I had no life vest and I was drugged!

I've got to climb out, I told myself. *Just don't black out!*

My arms felt like rubber. I latched onto a rock but my fingers wouldn't hold on, and I slipped away. It was all I could do to keep my face above water as the current pulled, pushed, and bounced me downstream like polar bears playing with a piece of blubber.

Come on, guys, lighten up, I muttered.

What was I doing—talking to imaginary polar bears? This was like a bad, bad dream.

Then I remembered the ocean. It couldn't be far. If I didn't get out soon, I would be swept out to sea.

The big white bears turned to great white sharks in my mind. I could see them coming up out of the deep, mouths open, teeth showing . . .

Whoa! Panic jolted me. I kicked my arms and legs toward shore. Please, just a little farther.

Then a growling piece of white water grabbed me and yanked me back into the rapids. Water filled my mouth, nose, and ears.

I sputtered and shook until I could halfway see. What I saw didn't make me happy. I was heading straight for a whirlpool, just under the bank! There was nothing I could do. I reached the edge of the pool and the suction began sweeping me around and around, slowly at first, then faster and faster. When I got to the center, I knew, I would go down like a cockroach flushed down the toilet!

"Help me!" I yelled above the roar. "Help!"

I reached the center. I began to go down. As my head went under I stuck my hand straight up. If only I could grab something!

Like a stick maybe? A stick! My hand felt it, for real! I grasped and held on—and something began tugging me upward.

Somebody was trying to save me!

I squeezed with all my might. Slowly I rose from the deadly funnel. Then my face burst out and I breathed deeply. I kicked and came free.

On the bank the gnome lay flat, holding to the other end of the long branch. With surprising strength he pulled me into still water and I climbed out onto the rocks, gasping and coughing.

When I finally caught my breath I sat up—but the gnome was gone.

Weird! But I was too wet, cold, and tired to figure it all out. And Ax! What happened to him? What if he didn't wake up like I did? He could be drowning!

I got up and staggered along the shore.

"Ax!" I yelled. "Ax! Where are you?"

I didn't have to look far. He was around the first bend, lying on his side. The gnome was bending over him.

"Ax!" I shouted. "Are you okay?"

The gnome looked up in alarm, then turned and scampered away like a mountain goat into the forest.

11

I knelt beside Ax.

His lips were blue. I felt the side of his neck. There was a pulse. I put my fingers under his nose. He was breathing—just cold and banged up, like me.

"Ax." I shook his shoulder gently.

He coughed. Then his eyelids fluttered open. "Eric. What happened?" He coughed some more.

Just then I heard the shrill cry of a hawk upstream. It sounded like a warning.

The person who had shot us—what if he was still looking for us?

I glanced around. Nearby lay a huge log, its twisted roots as tall as a man.

"Let's get under that log," I whispered, "in case

he comes back."

"In case who comes back?"

"No time to explain. Come on."

I helped him up, but the second his right foot touched the ground he crumpled.

"It's twisted!" he said.

The hawk screamed again, straight overhead. Something had spooked it and it was flying away. We had to hide—now!

I slipped my arm around Ax's back and we hobbled to the log. I pushed aside sticks and rocks and we climbed under, into the little hollow made where the trunk met the roots. I pulled some brush up to screen us.

"Would you tell me what's going on?" Ax said.

"Shhh!"

I heard the crunch of footsteps on gravel. Someone was walking along the stream.

"Don't move," I whispered to Ax.

His face showed pain, fear, and confusion. He had never seen the tranquilizer dart and still didn't know what had happened to us.

The footsteps drew closer. Whoever it was was taking his time, probably scanning the river to see if we washed up. As long as he stayed behind us we should be okay. If he came around front he might see us.

Please God, don't let him find us, I prayed.

I couldn't imagine what kind of madman would

sneak around the forest shooting people with tranquilizer darts.

The footsteps stopped, right behind the log. Then,
to my horror, they came around front. The man
walked right past us, never thinking to look over. It
probably didn't occur to him that we had survived.
He turned his back to us—and sat down on our log!
I could almost touch his mukluks.

Hey! Those boots sure looked familiar.

Then he lay his rifle gently on the ground. I
couldn't see his face but I saw his shirt: red-and-
black checkered . . .

Dwayne!

Ax and I stared at each other in shock. How did
he get here? What was he doing? And most of all—
why had he shot us?

In a few moments I heard the click of a cigarette
lighter, the hiss of the flame. Then I smelled pipe
tobacco, like vanilla and cherries mixed with burn-
ing rope.

Dwayne just sat there smoking. I had the feeling
he was watching to see if our bodies floated by.

The gun wasn't far away. If I moved quickly I
could grab it, roll out of the way, and come up
pointing!

No way. What if it wasn't even loaded? If Ax
were okay we could probably take the guy on, but
with Ax's foot twisted I'd be on my own. Dwayne
might overpower me—and then what?

I realized I was shivering. Maybe it was because I was so cold. I was soaked, and the air was chilly with drizzle. Or maybe it was sheer terror, as I waited to see what Dwayne was going to do.

I heard a gurgling noise as he sucked on his pipe. The hawk whistled, far away. The stream continued to roar and crash.

Finally Dwayne tapped his pipe against the log. Ashes showered onto the rocks. Then he stood, stretched, and walked away.

Hey! He left his rifle!

I was just starting to reach for it when he returned, muttering, "I'd forget my head if it wasn't screwed on . . ."

He never saw us. He turned and headed back the way he came. His footsteps crunched in the gravel as he walked up the creek, then faded as he stepped into the grass.

I looked at Ax. He was shivering too. It had to be the cold.

"Would you please tell me what is going on?" he whispered.

12

"We need to tell Miss Spice," Ax said after I explained.

"Can you walk?"

"With your help."

We crawled out from under the log. I helped him to his feet—or foot. He put his arm around my shoulders. We took a few steps.

Suddenly I slipped on a loose rock. "Whoa!" I said as we tumbled to the ground.

Ax grabbed his ankle and moaned. "Would you be careful?"

"Sorry. Maybe it's that tranquilizer."

"Let's try it again."

I helped him up. Leaning on my shoulders, he

hobbled along beside me. We made it to the grass, but as we climbed the short slope my foot slid in the mud. We landed on our faces.

"This is crazy!" Ax growled. "We'll never get back like this."

"If we could just get on level ground," I said.

"Level ground! What level ground? We've got to go over that hill to get back to camp."

I peered across the valley to the steep, wooded ridge. I remembered the zigzag trail, plus the mud, rocks, and logs.

"Maybe I should go get Miss Spice and the girls and bring them here," I said.

"And then what?"

"Maybe we could all carry you."

"You'd have to have a stretcher." He made a fist and struck the ground. "I *hate* this! I *hate* being helpless. And this is going to mess up my karate practice. I know a guy who sprained his ankle and it took, like, weeks to heal!"

"It's not *my* fault," I said.

"I know. It's that Dwayne guy. He must be nuts."

The rain, which had been drizzling softly, began to fall harder. Ax glanced up at the gray sky. "Man, I'm freezing."

He was shivering. I'd been so worried I hadn't thought much about being cold. Now I really felt it.

The air itself wasn't all that cold. It was the wet. Our clothes were soaked and getting worse by the minute. I remembered reading that if you were wet you could freeze to death even if the temperature was in the sixties.

"I wish we hadn't left the ponchos," I said.

"Maybe we should get back under that log," Ax said. "At least it'll block the rain. Then we can figure out what to do."

I nodded. He slipped his arm around my shoulder and we made our way back down to the big log, crawling underneath. It wasn't as dry as a tent, but it would do.

"When it stops raining we can try again," I said.

He shook his head. "Don't you remember what Meg said? It rains here most of the time. It may be days before it stops."

"Maybe we should stay here. Miss Spice and the girls will come looking."

"Yeah, but how will they find us? We're nowhere near the trail."

"Oh yeah," I said. "I wonder how far we floated."

He lay back and threw an arm across his face. "Who knows? I just wish I had some aspirin or something."

"For secret agents we're not very prepared," I said. "No ponchos, no first-aid kit. I don't even have any matches, do you?"

"No."

"It's cold and raining and you've got a hurt ankle," I went on. "This is a survival situation."

"We'll survive, buddy!" Ax growled. "I just don't know how yet."

We listened to the rain fall, tapping on the log and rocks. Drops plopped around us, hitting our feet and legs. At least it wasn't quite as cold under here, out of the wind. Even so, I was shivering.

"Well," I said finally. "I might as well go get Miss Spice. She'll know what to—"

"Shhh!" he hissed, sitting up suddenly. "Listen."

Footsteps—very soft, like someone sneaking.

Ax mouthed one word: "Dwayne."

He was coming from the other side. He must have circled around, then heard us talking.

The log creaked as he stepped quietly onto it. Ax picked up a rock. I grabbed a stick, but I was shaking so badly I could hardly hold onto it.

He must be directly overhead. There were no more footsteps now, just the plop of rain.

He leaped, and landed right in front of us. But when he stooped to peer under the log, we got a shock. This wasn't Dwayne—it was the gnome!

13

I had expected a fat little dude with a long beard. But this gnome was black, as in African-American. And he looked about my age, though it was hard to tell since he was so small. He was dressed in regular clothes: jeans, hiking boots, flannel shirt, green rainjacket—even an L.A. Lakers cap!

No, he wasn't a real gnome. He was a—what? As I stared into his eyes, I remembered my social studies book.

"You're a pygmy!" I exclaimed.

He grinned. Then he glanced up at the log and said something in a foreign language. To my surprise another pygmy jumped down—a girl!

"I am Benny, from the Ituri Forest in Africa," the

boy said in a French accent. "This is my sister, Sue."

Ax and I stared at each other, then burst out laughing.

"I'm sorry," I said when I caught my breath. "I mean—we thought you were gnomes."

"Yeah," Ax said. "We never expected to meet pygmies out here."

"Especially named Benny and Sue," I added.

"We will explain," Benny said. "But first you must come to our house."

"Your house?" I said.

"It is a tree," said the girl, who was just a little younger than her brother. She was cute too, even if she was tiny. She was dressed pretty much like her brother, only her cap said "California Dreaming."

"Why did you come back?" I asked Benny as Ax and I crawled out. "I mean, you ran away before."

"That man follows us," Benny answered. "I see him shoot you. He think you were us. I send Sue back to the tree, and I run for help. I pull you two out of the water, then I run because I am afraid of that man. I hide and watch him go. Then I see you hurt." He nodded at Ax's ankle. "So I find Sue to help."

"I help fix your foot," Sue said.

"Thanks a lot," Ax said.

I nodded. "Yeah. We're in a bind."

Ax put his left arm around my neck and his right hand on Benny's shoulder. With Sue leading the way, we began to travel.

We crossed the grassy valley and entered the forest. Before long we came to the biggest tree I had ever seen, big around as a small house.

"Welcome," Benny said.

I looked up, expecting to see a platform. The tree rose to the sky, but there was no shelter. Then Sue pulled aside some bushes at the base to reveal an opening. The tree was hollow! We stooped to go inside.

Sue lit a candle, and I stared in wonder at their "home." It was like a small cave except the walls were wood instead of stone. There was no ceiling, just a tunnel that went up into the darkness. On the ground lay a pair of sleeping bags, with small backpacks leaning beside them. Chunks of wood served as a table and stools.

"Sit," Sue said to Ax. "I find something for your foot. Benny, make some hot tea."

"Okay," he said as she went out.

Ax sat on a sleeping bag while Benny lit a camp stove and put on a small pot of water.

"This is incredible," I said.

"We are lucky," Benny said in his funny accent that made me think of a French detective.

"I don't get it," Ax said. "I mean, what are you guys doing here in these woods?"

Benny sat on a stool while the water heated. "Last year a man from Hollywood come to the Ituri Forest. He want to make a movie. He like my mother. So he asks her to come to America to be in other movies. Sue and I do not want to leave, but our parents say America is the land of opportunity. So we come to Hollywood and go to school—"

"How did you learn English so fast?" Ax asked.

"We learned from missionaries in Africa. But Sue and I hate Hollywood. We want to go home, but our parents won't let us. So we run away."

"Wait a minute," I said. "You mean you like the jungle better than Hollywood?"

"My parents have too much money now," Benny replied. "They drink. And then they fight. My father is angry because Mother makes all the money and he does not. So he beats her—and Sue and me too. Mother says she wants divorce, but still they stay together, always fighting."

"Can't they send you back to Africa to stay with the missionaries or something?" I asked.

"They won't. They say America is the promised land. But all the promises are lies."

"But how did you get *here*?" Ax asked. "We're a long way from Hollywood."

"We have a friend, a teenager. He can drive. He help us run away. First we go to Desolation Wilderness."

Ax and I stared at each other.

"We pick it because of the name," Benny said. "We think it not have people there. But someone saw us, and they tell the newspaper. Other newspapers picked up the story. Our friend saw the articles and came to get us. He take us here—the Lost Coast. We hoped a place named Lost Coast would have no people." He shook his head. "But there are people everywhere. It is not like the Ituri Forest."

Just then Sue pushed the bushes aside and came in. Tears streamed down her face.

"It is not good," she said. "I look everywhere for herbs, but I do not find any. It is not like the Ituri Forest. All the plants are different!"

"You see?" Benny said. "We are strangers in a strange land."

14

Water boiled in the pot. Benny turned the stove off, put tea bags in a pair of metal cups, and poured the water in. He handed the cups to Ax and me.

"Don't you guys want some?" I asked.

"Later. We have only two cups."

Sue wiped her eyes. "Let me see your foot," she said to Ax, kneeling beside him.

He nodded, then groaned as she removed his shoe. She peeled off the socks, and we saw that the ankle was swollen and bruised.

"Oh, man!" Ax said. "That'll never heal."

"Do not worry," Sue said. "See?" She pulled out a first-aid kit with a red cross on it.

I grinned at Ax.

Quick as a trained nurse, she unrolled a strip of bandage and wrapped Ax's ankle and foot.

"Aspirin?" Benny asked. He shook a couple of pills out of a bottle and handed them to Ax, who downed them with a sip of tea.

I sipped my tea too. It was hot and good. I pulled out the tea bag and laid it on the ground. I was starting to warm up inside this cozy tree.

"How do you get here?" Benny asked. "You do not have packs."

"We're camped in the next valley," I said. "We're with some other people."

"I wish Miss Spice was here now," Ax said. "She'd know how to help you guys."

Benny smiled. "You need help now. Not us."

I glanced at my watch. "Man, it's after noon. I wonder if they're looking for us yet."

"I doubt it," Ax said. "They probably won't get worried till later. Maybe you should go back and get them, Eric."

"We still won't have a way to get you over that hill," I said.

"Is no problem," Benny said. "Just follow the beach."

"Beach?" Ax asked.

He nodded. "It is not far, and I think it goes to your valley."

"Perfect!" Ax said, draining his tea. "Let's do it!"

"First, we eat," Benny said. He got some cheese

and crackers from a pack, then made tea for himself and Sue.

"What's it like in the Ituri Forest?" I asked.

Sue's eyes lit up. "Très bien! Beautiful forest. And many animals. Hippos ... monkeys ..."

"And warm," Benny said. "Not like here."

"Is it, like, mountains, or what?" Ax asked.

Benny shook his head. "Flat. Swamp. Big trees."

"It rains every day, but not cold rain," Sue said. She sipped her hot tea and took a bite of cracker. "I miss it so much!"

"You guys sure got a raw deal," Ax said, cracker crumbs dribbling down his chin.

"I wish I could think of some way to help," I said. "I don't think running away is the answer, though."

Sue nodded. "You are right. It is no good."

"But I am not going back to my father!" Benny said fiercely.

Sue put a hand on her brother's arm and spoke to him softly in their language. Ax and I looked at each other, wishing we could help.

When we finished eating, Sue blew out the candle and we went outside. Benny covered the opening to their tree. The rain had stopped falling, for now anyway.

Ax braced himself on Benny and me as Sue led the way. Soon I heard crashing surf. We came out at the end of the valley where the white-water stream flowed into the ocean.

"Where's the beach?" Ax asked. All we could see was boulders.

"To the left," Benny said.

It was hard getting past the rocks. When we got to the base of the cliff, though, I saw a narrow strip of gray sand.

Benny frowned. "It is small now."

"The tide's coming in, that's why!" Ax said over the roar of the waves.

"If the tide catches us before we get around, it will pound us into the cliffs," I said. "Then it'll wash us out to sea with the great white sharks."

"We can make it!" Ax said. "It can't be far."

"Maybe we should spend the night with them and try it tomorrow," I suggested.

Benny and Sue looked at each other uncertainly.

Ax scowled. "Come on, you guys! The longer we stand here arguing, the less time we have before the tide comes in."

Benny and Sue spoke in their language. Then Benny nodded. "All right. We go."

15

We walked along the beach, a rocky cliff towering on our left. On our right, waves crashed onto the sand, then slid back out, hissing like snakes. All around us lay boulders and washed-up logs.

"Look," Sue said, pointing to the cliff where pieces of driftwood were stuck in the rocks.

"It is bad," Benny said.

I stopped. "You mean that's where high tide gets?"

"Oh, that was just blown up by a storm," Ax said. "Come on."

We limped along. Every few seconds I glanced to see how close the waves were getting. Their mist touched my face, their salt tickled my nose, their boom shook my bones. They were loud as the landing strip at an airport.

"Not so fast!" Ax said. "I'm crippled, remember?"

"Sorry," I said. "I forgot." Fear made me walk fast. "How far do you think it is?"

"Can't be more than a mile, I'd say," Ax guessed.

"A mile! It was more than twice that on the trail," I said.

"Yeah, but there were switchbacks and everything. The beach is straight."

"Doesn't look too straight to me."

Actually, it curved outward. There was a big bend up ahead with the cliff jutting out almost to the water.

"Look!" Sue said. "Birds!"

We saw large pelicans skimming the waves, just missing the crests.

"Did you hunt back in Africa?" I asked.

"Children hunt birds," Benny said. "Adults hunt big game, like elephant."

"Wow!" Ax said. "With what, guns?"

Benny shook his head. "Spears."

"How do pygmies kill elephants with spears?" Ax asked. "I mean, no offense or anything, but elephants are huge!"

Benny nodded. "The elephant does not see us because we are small. The men can sneak up close. Then someone runs in and stabs it with a spear."

"Man, that's brave!" Ax said.

Benny shrugged. "The elephant does not die right

away. It runs away. But the men follow it until it goes down."

"What do you do with all that meat?" Ax asked.

Benny grinned. "We feast. And we sell some to tall people. They are not so good at hunting."

"I thought it was illegal to kill elephants," I said.

"Not in the Ituri Forest," Benny said. "We hunt them for food, not ivory. So we kill not so many."

"Listen!" Sue said. "Is it dogs?"

We stopped. It was hard to hear above the crash of the waves, but I could make out the sound of barking.

"Think it's a wild pack?" I asked.

"Probably some campers with pets," Ax said.

We kept trudging. As we reached the curve, spray drenched us.

"Man, those waves are getting close!" I said.

"We must hurry," Sue said.

But when she rounded the bend, she stopped suddenly.

"What is it?" Benny asked.

She pointed. As we came even with her, we saw a mass of brown bodies on the beach. Seals!

There were hundreds, maybe thousands. They covered the beach, stood on the rocks, swam in the surf, even perched part of the way up the cliff! They sounded like a giant dog pound.

Then *they* saw *us*.

First it was just one, a little guy. He started yapping and running away from us like a scared puppy.

Then one of the grown-ups looked over. She bared her teeth and sounded the alarm. Suddenly they were all staring at us—and they didn't seem happy with what they saw!

A big bull seal came rushing toward us. He must have weighed five hundred pounds. His fangs were bigger than a German shepherd's. And even though he had flippers instead of feet, he covered the ground surprisingly fast.

Sue and Benny ran for the cliff, climbing to safety. I didn't blame them. I would have done the same, but I remembered Ax couldn't run.

The other seals joined in the charge. Ax and I faced an army, and there was no way we could outrun them with his injury. All we could do was stand there.

"Uh—know any self-defense against seals?" I said.

"I could try something if it weren't for this ankle," he griped. "Like maybe a flying side kick to that big goon's throat."

"He'd eat you in one bite."

"I think you're right."

Our attackers were getting closer by the second, a brown tide of teeth and muscle.

"Run for it, Eric," Ax said. His voice was strangely calm, as if he felt ready to meet death. "Save yourself, buddy. There's no need for both of us to die."

I looked at him, then at the seals. I had to decide—and fast!

16

Then I remembered the pygmies. Those little-bitty guys, armed only with spears, taking on a herd of elephants.

If they could do it, so could I.

"Get back, you stupid seals!" I yelled. My voice was so loud it surprised even me. But it didn't surprise me as much as what happened next.

They stopped. All of them, except some in the back who must not have heard.

"Excuse me, Ax," I said, moving his arm off my shoulders. He sat down in the sand. I walked toward the crowd of seals, waving my arms. They looked angry but uncertain.

"I said get back!" I shouted.

They began to wallow away. It was like they decided we weren't worth fooling with.

"And I thought seals were smart!" Ax said.

"Me too." I couldn't believe it! My heart was racing, my hands shaking. That was all it took?

Benny and Sue scrambled down the cliff and ran over. They patted me on the back.

"You are brave!" Sue said.

"You are a good hunter," Benny said.

I really did feel proud then.

"Is it safe now?" Sue asked, staring at the mob, who acted as if they'd never seen us.

"Of course it's safe!" I declared. "They know who the boss is now."

"Don't get cocky," Ax said as Benny helped him up. "They might change their minds."

I grinned. "You're right. Let's make tracks."

The seals moved aside as we drew close but didn't pay us much attention. They didn't look fierce up close, except for a few of the big bulls, who ignored us. They were just like the seals I'd seen at a theme park, with big friendly eyes. They barked and grunted and yelped. Mothers groomed babies, and youngsters dove in the surf, which didn't bother them a bit. The bulls stood by themselves, looking tough. I knew now they were just bullies, like some kids I've known. They come up making noise and acting mean, but if you stand your ground they back down. When they charged, all the others

joined in without even knowing why.

"If our people were here, they would kill and eat," Benny said. "Our village has many fearless hunters."

"I'm glad they're *not* here," Sue said. "These seals are cute."

"Unless you're a fish," I said. "That's what they eat."

"They sure are good swimmers!" Ax said, admiring some playing in the huge waves like kids in a pool. "I don't see how they do it."

"Just look at those bodies," I said. "They're made for the water."

He nodded. "Soft. Blubbery. Slow-moving. Kind of like you, Eric." He grinned.

"Very funny!"

"You know I'm just joking. You stood beside me, buddy, and I won't forget it."

I smiled. I *did* feel proud. I didn't know those seals were bluffing when I yelled at them!

"You'd have done the same for me," I said.

Sue pointed down the beach. "Is that your stream?"

We saw an opening in the cliff walls, with trees, grass, and a creek.

"Has to be," Ax said.

"Look! I see someone!" Benny said.

I made out two colorful figures on the rocks near the stream mouth.

"I'll bet that's Sharon and Meg," I said.

We went as fast as we could, leaving the seals behind. I was eager to get back. After all, we had our "gnomes." Now I just wanted to get out of here—and away from that crazy Dwayne.

Sharon and Meg saw us. They jumped up and down and waved.

"They're probably afraid to come out because of the tide," Ax said, walking faster.

I'd forgotten it. Now I noticed the water sliding almost to our feet. It would just be a matter of minutes before the beach disappeared!

When we reached the stream, Sharon and Meg, wearing brightly colored ponchos, came running toward us.

"What on earth is going on?" Sharon asked, looking relieved to see us.

Then she and Meg stared at the pygmies.

Ax cleared his throat. "Sharon and Meg, I want you to meet our new friends, Benny and Sue. Otherwise known as the Little People of the Lost Coast."

"You mean . . . ?" Sharon began.

I nodded. "That's right. They're the gnomes, live and in person."

Meg noticed Ax's bandage. "What happened to your ankle?" she asked him.

"Twisted," he said.

"Let's see." She knelt to examine it. "Somebody did a good job of bandaging it."

"Sue did that," Ax said.

Meg shot an admiring glance at Sue. "Well, come on," she said, slipping her arm around Ax's back. "I'll help you."

17

"Where's Miss Spice?" I asked when we got to camp.

"She's looking for you guys," Sharon said. "We were at the beach watching for seals when we saw you."

Ax sat on the ground and stretched his leg out. The rest of us sat on rocks and logs. "Well, did you see any?" he said.

Sharon shook her head. "I guess there just aren't any around."

Ax glanced at me with a grin. He was about to tell her, but Meg interrupted: "So what's the story? Are Benny and Sue really gnomes?"

We quickly explained.

"Wait a minute," Meg said to Benny and Sue. "You mean you're the ones that were in the Desolation Wilderness?" She shook her head. "I don't get it."

Sue smiled. "That was us. But people saw us, so we come here. A friend brought us." Her smile faded. "Then that man found us."

"What man?" Sharon said.

"Dwayne," I said. "He's the one—"

"I'm the one who shot you," said a man's voice. To my horror Dwayne stepped out from behind a tree. He wore the same red and black hunting shirt, purple hat, and mukluks. And he carried a rifle. "It was an accident. I admit it, and I'm sorry," he said.

"*Shot* them?" Sharon said.

He patted his gun. "Tranquilizer darts. I was tracking our gnomes here when I saw these two boys. I just assumed they were the gnomes. I was far away and couldn't tell the difference, you see. So I shot." He shrugged. "I had no idea you boys would fall in the river." He grinned. "Sorry."

"But why did you want to shoot the gnomes—I mean the pygmies—in the first place?" Ax asked with a frown.

"I prefer the word gnomes," Dwayne said, reminding me once again of a school teacher. "Or perhaps some new word yet to be invented."

"But you heard what they said," I said. "They're African pygmies, that's all. The gnome business was a simple mix-up."

Dwayne shook his head like I'd given a wrong answer in class. "That remains to be seen. I won't know for sure until I get them in the laboratory."

"Laboratory!" Sue said. I felt a cold chill down my spine.

Benny moved close to his sister. "Who are you anyway, Mister?" he asked.

"Dwayne Burpson, B.S., M.S., soon to be Ph.D.," Dwayne said. "I'm working on my doctorate in zoology."

"Zo-what?" I said.

"The study of animals," Sharon whispered.

"The discovery of a new species of primate would do wonders for my career." Dwayne grinned again.

"I get it," Ax said. "You were going to tranquilize Benny and Sue and take them back to your lab for tests, all so you could become famous."

"That's why we didn't black out completely," I said, snapping my fingers. "The tranquilizer dosage was for people smaller than us."

Dwayne nodded, as if I'd finally figured out the answer to a math problem. "Good thinking, young man. As for you"—he nodded at Ax—"You're completely off base. Scholars like myself have no interest in anything as vulgar as fame. I'm concerned with our understanding of the natural world." He raised a finger. Lecture time. "Science—a candle in the darkness. If I can shine just a little light into the

92

dark ignorance of our world, I'll be satisfied." He shrugged. "And if I happen to be recognized as the leader in my field, well, who am I to complain?"

"Yeah, but you want to treat Benny and Sue like lab rats!" Sharon protested.

"Not at all," Dwayne said. "They'll have food, shelter, clothing. What more could they want?"

"We are not animals!" Benny said. "And you are not taking us."

"We'll see about that," Dwayne said, pointing his gun at Benny.

He was wearing a fanny pack, and he slid it around, unzipped it, and pulled out a coiled rope. "Here, little girl." He tossed it to Sharon. "Tie this around the female's waist, then the male's."

"No way!" Sharon said, dropping the rope. "This is outrageous!"

Dwayne scowled, moving the gun barrel in Sharon's direction.

"Wait," said Meg, who had been deep in thought. "He's got a gun, Sharon. We might as well do what he says." She reached down, picked up the rope, and knotted it around Sue, then Benny.

"Now, tie that end around *my* waist," Dwayne said. As Meg approached, pulling Benny and Sue, Dwayne laughed. "There won't be any escapes this time."

18

Dwayne raised his arms so Meg could tie the rope around his waist. But she pointed at his empty hand.

"Is that a cut?" she asked.

He frowned. "What?"

"Let me see your hand," Meg said, sounding like a concerned nurse.

He held it out, and she took it by the wrist. Then, suddenly, she twisted it to the side. To my amazement, Dwayne did a sideways flip, landing on his back! So that's what Meg was planning.

"Aikido!" Ax said. "Yes!"

Before I could go for the gun, Dwayne got to his feet and lunged at Meg. She grabbed his arm again, but this time Dwayne pivoted and it was Meg who went flying, hitting the ground with an "oof!"

"Judo! Yes!" Dwayne said, snatching up the gun. "I took it in college," he added with a mean grin.

"You knocked the wind out of her," Ax said, pointing to Meg, who lay gasping. "Somebody raise her arms so she can breathe."

Dwayne glanced at me and nodded, and I hurried to Meg's side. I raised her arms above her head and she inhaled. In a few moments she gasped, "I'm okay."

Meanwhile Dwayne knotted the rope around his own waist, then pulled some cord from his fanny pack and tied Benny and Sue's hands behind their backs.

"Enough chitchat," Dwayne said. "We've got ground to cover."

He began walking up the trail, Benny and Sue stumbling behind, tugged by the rope. They looked back at us with pleading eyes, but there was nothing we could do.

When they were out of sight, Sharon dashed to Miss Spice's pack.

"What are you doing?" Ax said. "This is no time for a snack!"

Sharon pulled out a map. "I want to find out where they're going; maybe we can head them off."

"You don't think we should wait till Miss Spice gets back?" I said.

"No time," Sharon answered.

Meg, sitting up now, frowned. "I don't under-stand why they went that way. The trailhead park-ing lot is in the other direction."

"Here's why!" Sharon said, pointing at the map, which she had spread on the ground. "Look. A log-ging road comes in close to the trail."

The rest of us gathered around.

"Hey, that's the ridge that overlooks the valley where we got shot!" Ax said.

"Looks like you can turn up it and come to the logging road," Sharon said.

"Yeah, but it's miles from there to a paved road," I noted.

"I'll bet he's got four-wheel drive," Meg said. "He's probably parked there."

"Look," Sharon said. "If we cut straight across here, through this valley, we can head him off."

"What about Ax?" Meg said.

"I'll stay here. I'll be fine," he said. "Miss Spice will be back soon."

"Why don't you stay with him, Meg?" Sharon suggested.

Meg nodded. "I'm kind of sore anyway."

"You sure you're all right?" Ax asked her, and she nodded again.

"Eric, you and I can go," Sharon said. She traced her finger on the map. "If we go straight through here, fast, we might get to his vehicle before he does."

"If that's where he is," I said. "We're just guessing."

"Do you have a better idea?" she said impatiently, folding the map and sticking it in her hip pocket. "If he escapes, we may never see Benny and Sue again!"

I nodded. "Let's go."

"You guys be careful," Meg said.

"But not too careful," Ax added.

Sharon and I set off up the trail at a jog. When we topped the rise, she turned right into the woods. We ran down the side of the ridge into a hollow. After we'd gone a half mile or so she stopped to study the map.

"It should be right up there," she said, pointing up a steep, wooded slope.

"We've got to be quiet," I said.

We scrambled up the hill under tall trees that smelled of mint. The mossy ground muffled our footsteps. At the top of the ridge we crouched behind some bushes. There lay the logging road. To our right was a big maroon pickup truck with fat, knobby tires. Beside it stood a large green tent. No one was around.

"Perfect!" Sharon whispered. "We beat them here."

"Now what?"

"Listen! I hear voices. We've got to hurry," she said, frowning.

"I know, let's get inside the tent," I said. "When he steps in we can throw a sleeping bag over his head."

"Good idea," Sharon said.

We sprinted down the logging road and ducked into the tall, dark tent, which was unzipped. My heart pounded not only from the exercise but from the sound of approaching footsteps. Sharon and I stared at each other as we heard them walk into camp.

19

"I'm going to tie you to the truck while I break camp," Dwayne said to Benny and Sue.

Realizing he would be at the tent in moments, I looked around for a sleeping bag to throw over his head. There was nothing. He had already packed! Sharon and I stared at each other in horror.

Then everything went black!

It took me a second to realize Dwayne was taking down the tent. The fabric was collapsing around Sharon and me. I grabbed her arm and pulled her flat.

Suddenly Sue screamed. "Snake! A big one!"

"Where?" Dwayne said, running over.

I took that instant to find the opening and slide

out, Sharon behind me. Dwayne had his back to us. He bent over, peering under the truck where Sue pointed. Benny, though, was watching us. Somehow he and his sister must have known we were in the tent and pretended there was a snake to distract Dwayne.

Sharon tugged my sleeve and pointed at the tent. I nodded. We each grabbed a corner, tiptoed to the truck, and tossed it over Dwayne.

"What the—!" he yelled.

While he thrashed about, I snatched up the rifle. "Jump back, everybody!"

Dwayne threw off the big cloth. He was red-faced with fury. Then he saw the gun, aimed straight at his chest.

"I will shoot," I said. "I know it's a tranquilizer rifle, but there's enough in one of those darts to slow you down."

Dwayne relaxed. He even grinned. "It's not loaded."

"Right," I said. "You threatened us with it, remember?"

"I unloaded it when we came into camp. Safety precaution."

I glanced at Benny and Sue. They shrugged and frowned.

Dwayne took a step toward me. "Sorry," he said, holding out his hand for the rifle. "Nice try, though."

I looked through the scope, placing the crosshairs on his chest. I flipped the safety off and began to tighten my finger on the trigger.

Dwayne just smiled. He wasn't fooling.

I squeezed anyway. Expecting a dry click, I was surprised when the gun kicked and a metal syringe shot into Dwayne's chest.

"Ouch!" He stared at it in surprise. "I could have sworn I unloaded that gun," he said, shaking his head. "I'd forget my head if it wasn't . . ."

As I lowered the weapon, his knees wobbled and he reached for the truck. Then he slumped to the ground, sprawling on his back.

"Yay, Eric!" Sharon said, running over to hug me.

I grinned as we untied Benny and Sue, who hugged Sharon and me and jumped up and down with joy.

"Now what?" I said.

"Better find another cartridge, in case he comes to," Sharon said.

I found some extras in the glove compartment and reloaded. Just then we heard footsteps, and Miss Spice came running down the logging road at top speed.

"Wow! She should be in the Olympics!" I said.

Our boss slid to a halt, her face as red as her hair. "Everybody okay?" she asked, panting. "Ax and Meg told me where to find you."

"We're fine," Sharon said.

"I'll say," I added. "We've got our two gnomes, only they're not really gnomes, plus we've captured a gnome-hunter."

Dwayne groaned, coming to.

"Is he all right?" Miss Spice asked.

"Tranquilizer dart, light dose," I said. "He'll probably be up and around in a few minutes."

"Maybe we should tie him," Sharon suggested.

She and Miss Spice teamed up, binding Dwayne's hands and feet tightly.

"What are you doing?" he grumbled. Then he stared at Miss Spice. "I don't know who you are, but you're confining me against my will, and that's against the law."

I burst out laughing. "Against the law? What about you?"

Miss Spice put her hands on her hips. "Let me get this straight," she said to Dwayne, who twisted around on his side. "You shoot two children with tranquilizer darts, causing them to fall into a white-water river. Then you kidnap Benny and Sue here. Those sound like felonies to me, sir."

"The shooting was sheer accident," Dwayne argued, managing to sit up with his back against the truck. "I admitted that already and apologized to the boys. I thought they were gnomes—an honest mistake. And as for kidnapping, we have no proof as yet that these two gnomes even qualify as human. I'm betting they're a new species of primate."

"So how come they talk?" Sharon said.

"Even parrots can do that," Dwayne retorted.

"You see?" Sue exclaimed. "This is why I want to go back to the Ituri Forest. Everywhere we go, we are freaks. Gnomes! Leprechauns! Now this man thinks we're a new species."

Miss Spice put her arm around Sue's shoulders and stared at Dwayne thoughtfully. "You know, this sounds like extremely unprofessional behavior for a scientist. You are a scientist, aren't you?"

"I am!" Dwayne said proudly.

"Are you with a university?"

"Central California Community College, actually."

"Central Cal." She nodded. "Oh, I forgot to mention. I'm Jane Spice, director of Wildlife Special Investigations, a branch of the CIA. I'm acquainted with quite a number of leading biologists, and I wonder if they would approve of your methods. Shooting children with tranquilizer darts, for instance."

For the first time, Dwayne looked afraid. "It's all for the sake of science."

"Is that right?" Miss Spice said. "Well, we'll see about that. I think I may have a talk with the college officials."

Dwayne looked at the ground. He had come here for fame and fortune. Now he was tied up and about to be in trouble with federal and academic officials. I think he was finally beginning to realize his career was over.

20

There were only a few hours of daylight left, so we had to hurry. Leaving Miss Spice to guard Dwayne, the rest of us jogged back to camp. Ax and Meg were sitting side by side talking quietly. They obviously weren't mad at each other anymore.

"Did you get him?" Ax asked as we arrived.

I grinned and gave him a thumbs-up. "He's tied up, with Miss Spice watching."

"What happened?" Meg asked, shaking back her pretty brown hair.

I told them about hiding in the tent, which fell in on us. Sue told them that she and Benny had seen our footprints as soon as they came into camp, and that's why she'd yelled "Snake!" "Dwayne is so dumb," she giggled. "He did not see anything."

"Now we need to pack everything up and get back over there," I said. "We can drive out in Dwayne's truck and go get our van. It's not that far, Ax. You can lean on me."

"What about Benny and Sue?" Meg asked.

They looked down. "We'd better go back to our treehouse," Benny mumbled.

"Are you crazy?" I said. "You should get your packs and come with us."

"That would be crazy," Sue said. "Can't you see? There's no place for us in your world. There are too many Dwaynes around."

"Miss Spice will help," Ax said.

"Yeah, she'll think of something," I agreed.

"I'll try," said a voice in the woods.

"Miss Spice!" we shouted as she strode briskly down the trail carrying the rifle.

"Did he get away?" Ax asked in alarm.

Miss Spice smiled grimly as she came into camp. "I let him go."

"Let him go!"

"But why?" I asked.

"He poses no threat to us now." She patted the rifle. "Besides, I've got you kids to think about, especially Ax with his ankle. I just don't see how we could get Dwayne to a police station."

"But he's getting away with it," Ax said.

"Oh, no," Miss Spice said. "I know all I need to

106

know about Dwayne Burpson. I assure you, when we get out of here I'll see to it that he never works as a scientist again. I'll also look into the possibility of bringing criminal charges."

I was outraged. But she might be right about the difficulty of getting Dwayne to a police station, at least tonight. And if we didn't get him there tonight, we'd have to take turns standing guard all night with the gun . . .

Maybe she was right after all. She could track him down later. Heck, he probably wouldn't even try to flee, since he claimed he'd done nothing wrong.

"So how are we going to get out of here with Ax's hurt ankle?" I asked. "It's a long way to the parking lot."

"And what about Benny and Sue?" Sharon added.

"Yes, what about Benny and Sue?" Miss Spice said, eyeing the two pygmies curiously. "There's a lot I don't know here."

Trying not to talk all at once, we kids filled Miss Spice in on the whole story, or at least the main parts. I never got a chance to mention my standoff with the seals. Benny and Sue described their problems in Hollywood and how they wanted more than anything to go back to Africa.

"We told them you could help," I reminded Miss Spice.

"And I said I'd try, didn't I?" She smiled and

shook her head, then glanced at the sky. "Meanwhile, it's getting dark. I'd say it's obvious we're not leaving here tonight. As I understand it, Benny and Sue, your packs are in the other valley?"

They nodded.

"Do you have time to get them and be back here by dark?"

I answered for them. "The tide is too high now. They would have to take the long way."

"Tell you what," Miss Spice said. "You two go on back tonight and let me think about all this. In the morning maybe I'll have an answer. If not, or if you don't like my answer, fine. Stay out here as long as you like. But who knows? I just might come up with something."

They agreed to her proposal, said good-bye, and left. Then we got busy with supper before bedding down for the night.

In the morning when we woke up, Miss Spice was already cooking breakfast. I could tell by the way she was humming that she felt happy.

"Morning, everyone," she said as we came out of our tents.

"Morning," we said, yawning and stretching.

"You must have figured out some answers," Sharon said.

Miss Spice grinned. "One or two, anyway."

"What are they?" I asked.

"Let's wait till Benny and Sue get here."

108

"What if they don't show?"

"Oh, I have a feeling they will."

She was right, as usual. They arrived after breakfast, wearing their backpacks. Even though the packs were small, they looked huge on their pint-sized bodies.

"Hello, everybody," Sue said. She sounded nervous, as if not sure they'd made the right decision.

"Have you eaten?" Miss Spice asked.

They nodded.

"All right, then. Gather round, everybody, and let's have a good, old-fashioned powwow."

21

"In the old days, when American Indians had a powwow, they always started off by giving presents to their visitors," Miss Spice said as we sat around the ashes of the campfire. "So I have some gifts for *our* visitors."

She went to her pack and came back with her Bible. "Meg, this is for you. This is the one I always take camping, because it's lightweight. And just in case your mom is concerned about negative energy, I'm going to put some very positive energy into it."

She took a pen and wrote on the first page. "To Meg," she said, "my sweet, brave young cousin. I hope you enjoy this book as much as I have. Love, Aunt Jane."

She handed the book to Meg.

"Thanks, Aunt Jane." Meg said. "I've never had one of my own."

"You'll like it," Sharon whispered. "I read mine all the time."

"Now, for Benny and Sue," Miss Spice said. She went back to her pack and pulled out a plastic bag. "Fire starters," she said, holding it up. "Perfect for wet conditions."

"Thank you!" Sue said, taking the bag.

Ax frowned. "Why give them that if you don't want them to stay out here?"

Miss Spice sat on a log. "Actually, I had somewhere else in mind."

Benny frowned. "Not Hollywood?"

Miss Spice laughed. "Not Hollywood."

"The Ituri Forest?" Sue said hopefully.

"I'm afraid not," Miss Spice said. "Not if your parents forbid it."

"Where?" Sharon asked.

"A place similar in some ways to the Ituri Forest. A place that's hot and rainy, where those fire starters will come in handy. A place with alligators and swamps and—"

"The Everglades?" I guessed.

Miss Spice nodded. "That's it."

Sharon frowned. "But why send them to live in the middle of a swamp?"

"Not in the middle, dear," Miss Spice said. "I

111

have some friends who run a school near the Florida Everglades. It teaches all the usual subjects. And in their spare time the students and teachers explore the area."

"Cool!" Ax said.

"They learn all about the wildlife, and about wilderness survival," Miss Spice said.

"We would get to go into the forest?" Sue said.

"And look for alligators?" Benny added.

Miss Spice nodded.

"What about elephants?" Benny asked.

Miss Spice laughed. "Not in the Everglades, I'm afraid. But the Miami Zoo isn't too far from there, and they may have some."

Benny and Sue looked at each other. They talked in their own language. Then they smiled.

"It is good," Sue said.

"Better than here," Benny said, gesturing. "And better than Hollywood."

"When we get out, I'll talk with your parents," Miss Spice said. "The school is fully accredited, and it's in the United States. I think it might be just the answer."

"I bet Benny and Sue will know more about the swamp than the teachers," Ax said.

"It's very possible," Miss Spice agreed.

"So what about Ax?" I asked. "How are we going to get him out of here?"

Miss Spice's smile faded. "I'm afraid we'll have to

rely on sheer determination." She shrugged. "I guess we'll take turns helping him walk, unless somebody has a better idea."

We all stared at each other. Ax didn't look happy, but I could tell by the look on his face he was prepared to tough it out.

"Well, let's pack up," Miss Spice said. "Then we'll give it a try."

We began getting everything ready for the hike back. The packs were almost loaded when we heard voices. It sounded like a big group of kids.

"Wonder who that is," Miss Spice said, shielding her brow for a view.

Soon we saw them coming down the side of the hill, all dressed in green.

"Boy Scouts," Sharon said.

They made a lot of noise—talking, laughing, whistling, singing, whooping.

"They're louder than a herd of elephants," Benny said, and Sue giggled.

They were almost at the creek when one spotted us. "Hey!" he called back. "There's somebody camped up here!"

The group fell quiet, for a few seconds anyway. Then they resumed talking in low voices as they crossed the creek and arrived at our site. There must have been thirty boys our age and older, plus a couple of men.

"Good morning," said a man with a dark mustache.

"Sorry to disturb you."

"No problem," Miss Spice said with a smile. "We were just leaving."

"I'm Steve Box. I'm supposed to be in charge of this gang."

"Jane Spice."

"Nice campsite you have. Hey, boys! Want to camp here?"

"No!" they shouted.

"We want to find the gnomes," one said. They obviously didn't suspect Benny and Sue, although some of the boys were looking at them curiously.

The other man, who had reddish-blond hair, shushed them. "How are we going to find gnomes with everybody yelling?"

"So you're gnome-hunting?" Miss Spice said.

Steve Box grinned. "You might say that. We read about them in the paper. I'm not sure what our chances are of finding one with this crowd."

"Can I speak to you a moment in private?" Miss Spice said.

"Sure."

They stepped several feet away. She talked in a low voice. Steve Box glanced at Benny and Sue, then at Ax. He nodded.

"Boys, we've got a crisis," he said when they finished. "Who's working on a first-aid merit badge?"

A couple of hands shot up.

The Scout leader pointed to Ax. "This young man

has a sprained ankle. We need a stretcher, pronto. And some strong backs to carry him back to the parking lot."

"Uh, sir, what about the gnomes?" a boy asked.

"Ah, yes, the gnomes," Steve Box said. "First let's take care of this young man, then we'll talk about gnomes. I have a feeling they're not far from here. Not far at all."

22

That afternoon we had the North Coast Ice Cream and Pastry Shop all to ourselves. We sat around one big table, we kids eating ice cream, the women drinking coffee with whipped cream on top.

"Jane, it sounds like you've got a busy week coming up," Sarah said.

Miss Spice nodded. "First I've got to get Sharon and Eric to the airport tomorrow. Then take Benny and Sue to Hollywood and talk to their parents."

"And put *us* on a plane to Florida," Benny said.

"To the Everglades," Sue added.

"And take care of Dwayne," Ax said. "Like have him thrown in jail, I hope."

"We'll see," Miss Spice said. "I'm going to call

the local newspaper soon. Is everybody ready for interviews and photos?"

We nodded.

"I thought you guys would be more excited than that," Sarah said.

"I suspect they're worn out," Miss Spice said. "I know I am."

"At least we'll straighten out the gnome mystery," I said.

"Yes, and people will stop chasing us," Benny said.

"Next you can solve the mystery of Bigfoot," Sarah said. "Every once in a while somebody claims to see one."

"Maybe they're Nephilim," Meg said.

"What?" Sarah said.

"Nephilim. Giants. They're in the Bible."

Miss Spice put a hand on Sarah's arm. "I hope you don't mind. I gave Meg my Bible."

Meg peered at her mother, worried about her reaction. But Sarah smiled. "How thoughtful, Jane! I'm sure she'll enjoy it."

"But Mom, I thought you said it has too much negative energy," Meg said.

Sarah glanced at Miss Spice. "Children do remember things, don't they? I may have said that once, Meg. But I suppose if there's any negative energy in this old world, it's in people like Dwayne."

"And if there's any positive energy, it's in people like Meg," Miss Spice said.

117

"Yeah," Ax said. "You should have seen her throw Dwayne. She was awesome!"

Meg looked down, embarrassed but pleased.

"You should see Eric hunt seals," Sue said with a grin. "He is awesome too."

"Seals? What seals?" Sarah asked.

"This is the first I've heard about it," Miss Spice said.

All eyes were on me.

"Tell them," Ax said.

I set down my spoon. "Well, it was like this . . ."

Don't miss any of these great adventures from the Eric Sterling, Secret Agent series

The Secret of Lizard Island, Book 1
ISBN: 0-310-38251-3

Eric Sterling knows the Wildlife Special Investigations (WSI) branch of the CIA has gotten the wrong guy. But WSI doesn't listen when 12-year-old Eric tries to tell them. Instead, WSI sends Eric off on a mission to a remote South Sea island. Can an everyday kid like Eric complete a mission for the CIA involving renegade scientists that are using genetic engineering to breed giant lizards? And who is the Erik Sterling the CIA had wanted in the first place? Find out in the first adventure of this incredible series!

Double-Crossed in Gator Country, Book 2
ISBN: 0-310-38261-0

Eric and his two secret-agent sidekicks find themselves in the Everglades on an important mission for WSI. But what or who's going to get them first? The mosquitoes . . . the gators . . . the poisonous snakes . . . the ghost of the mysterious Mr. Watson . . . or the gun-wielding criminals who are illegally butchering alligators that Eric and the team have been sent to the Everglades to stop? Surrounded by more dangers than he can count, Eric has a job to do before he can get safely home. Surely he can trust the WSI agents in the big swamp to help him—can't he? Read all about it and experience the adventure with Eric!

Night of the Jungle Cat, Book 3
ISBN: 0-310-38271-8

Eric thought that as a special investigator for WSI he is supposed to help wildlife. Then why is WSI training him to use firearms and sending him alone to Central America with instructions to find and kill a rare black jaguar? Why not just trap it and put it into a zoo? And why was Eric sent on this assignment alone without his fellow agents, Erik K. and Sharon? The pieces will come together as you read this exciting adventure!

Smugglers on Grizzly Mountain, Book 4
ISBN: 0-310-38281-5

Eric and his special agent friends are afraid they'll freeze to death in Alaska. But WSI sends them there anyway to backpack into Denali National Park and find a ring of smugglers who've been taking vast numbers of mushrooms out of the park illegally, endangering the ecosystem. But when their contact at the base of the mountain mysteriously disappears, Eric hikes down the mountain to investigate and walks right into an ambush! Can Eric survive being kidnapped by dangerous smugglers and being threatened by grizzly bears? You won't want to miss the ending to this mystery!

Sisters of the Wolf, Book 5

ISBN: 0-310-20729-0

Kayaking into the swampy interior of Horn Island to check on the disappearance of protected red wolves, Eric and his partners fall into the clutches of two sinister, peculiar sisters. As the young agents are imprisoned in a spooky old house in the heart of the backwater wilds, they wonder whether they're dealing with something that could make even wolfnappers look tame. Find out if faith can help Eric and the gang conquer their worst fears.

Trouble at Bamboo Bay, Book 6

ISBN: 0-310-20730-4

Eric's Hawaiian vacation leads to far more than he ever dreamed: drugs, deadly cobras, and hand-to-hand combat with a young sniper! Why would a girl be training her sights on hikers in a state park? When he follows the sharpshooting Lana to her home, Eric not only discovers a tropical valley as beautiful as the Garden of Eden, but also that this valley has a "serpent" of its own: a drug dealer who thinks nothing of destroying this paradise to get what he wants. Follow the investigation to the end and find out if Eric and Lana stop him before he stops them . . . permanently. And can God's love turn Lana from serving Pele, the volcano goddess, to serving Jesus Christ?

Deathbird of Paradise, Book 7

ISBN: 0-310-20732-0

Eric is off to Papua, New Guinea on his latest investigation for WSI to catch poachers who are shooting endangered species. To track the villain down in the rain forest, Eric enlists the help of missionary friends, native bearers, and two sidekicks from previous adventures. But the poacher is pretty wily, so Eric and the team have to seek some unusual help from a huge, flightless bird! You'll never believe how this one ends!

ZondervanPublishingHouse

Grand Rapids, Michigan

http://www.zondervan.com

A Division of HarperCollins*Publishers*

We want to hear from you. Please send your comments about
this book to us in care of the address below. Thank you.

ZondervanPublishingHouse
Grand Rapids, Michigan 49530
http://www.zondervan.com